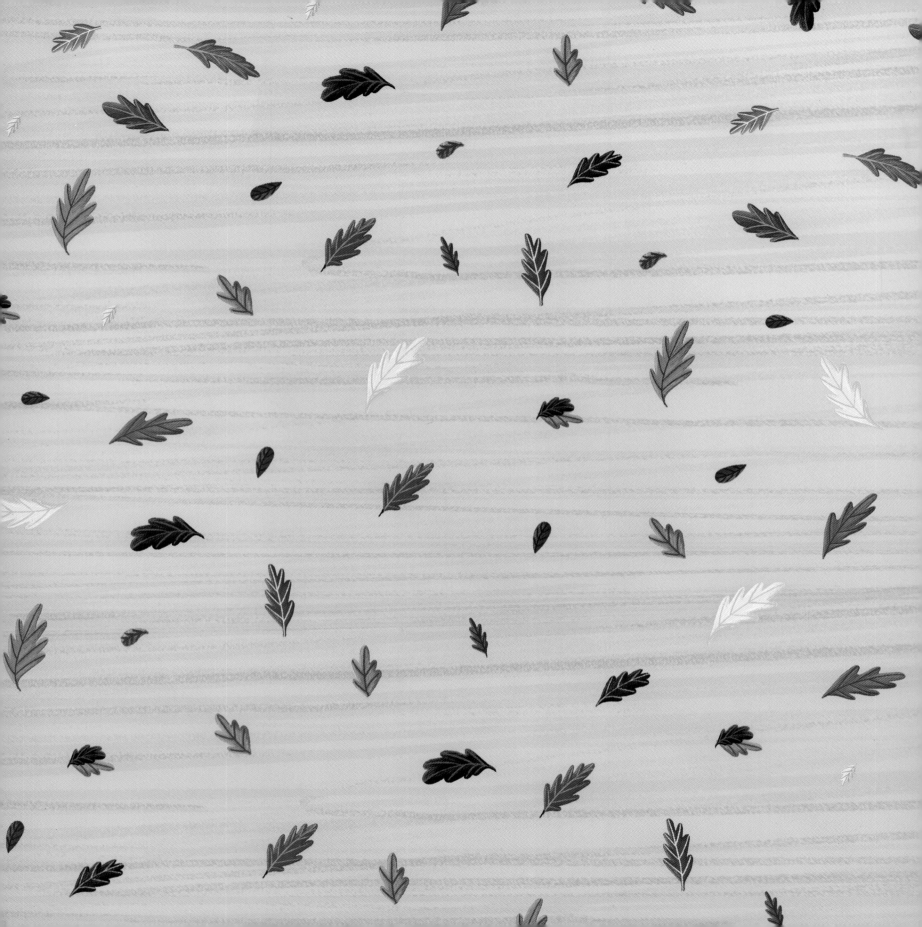

IMAGINE THAT™

Licensed exclusively to Imagine That Publishing Ltd
Tide Mill Way, Woodbridge, Suffolk, IP12 1AP, UK
www.imaginethat.com
Copyright © 2016 Imagine That Group Ltd
All rights reserved
2 4 6 8 9 7 5 3 1
Manufactured in China

Adapted by Oakley Graham
Illustrated by Kimberley Barnes

ISBN 978-1-78700-472-6

A catalogue record for this book is available from the British Library

Chicken Little

Adapted by Oakley Graham

Illustrated by Kimberley Barnes

As Chicken Little was walking in the woods one day,

'Plop!' an acorn fell from a tree on to his head.

'Help!' cried Chicken Little,
'The sky is falling down!

I must go and tell the king.'

Chicken Little raced off to find the king,

and met Henny Penny ...

'Where are you going, Henny Penny?' said Chicken Little.

'I'm going to the woods,' Henny Penny replied.

'No, Henny Penny, don't go there!'
said Chicken Little. 'The sky is falling down!

I'm going to tell the king.'

So Henny Penny joined Chicken Little, and off they went
to tell the king that the sky was falling down.

On the way they met Cocky Locky ...

'Where are you going, Cocky Locky?' said Henny Penny.
'I'm going to the woods,' Cocky Locky replied.

'No, Cocky Locky, don't go there! I was going to the woods when I met Chicken Little, and Chicken Little had been in the woods, and the sky was falling down!

We're going to tell the king.'

So Cocky Locky joined Henny Penny and Chicken Little,
and off they went to tell the king that the sky was falling down.

On the way they met Ducky Lucky ...

'Where are you going, Ducky Lucky?' said Cocky Locky.
'I'm going to the woods,' Ducky Lucky replied.

'No, Ducky Lucky, don't go there! I was going to the woods when I met Henny Penny, and Henny Penny had met Chicken Little, and Chicken Little had been in the woods, and the sky was falling down!

We're going to tell the king.'

So Ducky Lucky joined Cocky Locky and Henny Penny and Chicken Little, and off they went to tell the king that the sky was falling down.

On the way they met Drakey Lakey ...

'Where are you going, Drakey Lakey?' said Ducky Lucky.
'I'm going to the woods,' Drakey Lakey replied.

'No, Drakey Lakey, don't go there! I was going to the woods when I met Cocky Locky, and Cocky Locky had met Henny Penny, and Henny Penny had met Chicken Little, and Chicken Little had been in the woods, and the sky was falling down!

We're going to tell the king.'

So Drakey Lakey joined Ducky Lucky and Cocky Locky and Henny Penny and Chicken Little, and off they went to tell the king that the sky was falling down.

On the way they met Goosey Loosey ...

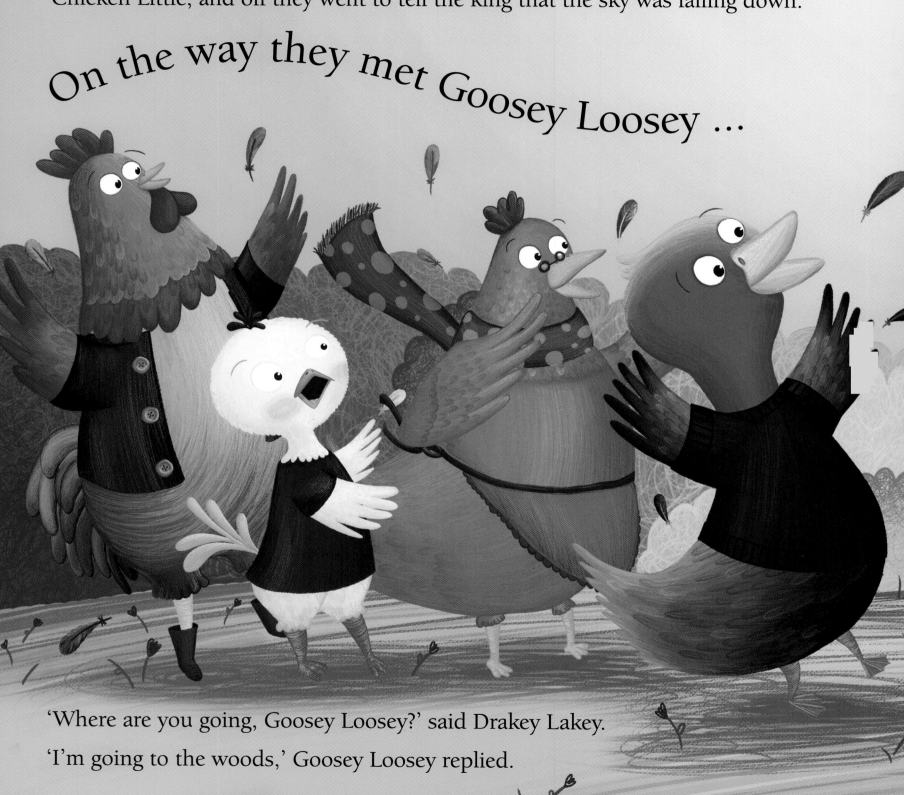

'Where are you going, Goosey Loosey?' said Drakey Lakey.

'I'm going to the woods,' Goosey Loosey replied.

'No, Goosey Loosey, don't go there! I was going to the woods when I met Ducky Lucky, and Ducky Lucky had met Cocky Locky, and Cocky Locky had met Henny Penny, and Henny Penny had met Chicken Little, and Chicken Little had been in the woods, and the sky was falling down!

We're going to tell the king.'

So Goosey Loosey joined Drakey Lakey and Ducky Lucky and Cocky Locky and Henny Penny and Chicken Little, and off they went to tell the king that the sky was falling down.

On the way they met Gander Lander …

'Where are you going, Gander Lander?' said Goosey Loosey.

'I'm going to the woods,' Gander Lander replied.

'No, Gander Lander, don't go there! I was going to the woods when I met Drakey Lakey, and Drakey Lakey had met Ducky Lucky, and Ducky Lucky had met Cocky Locky, and Cocky Locky had met Henny Penny, and Henny Penny had met Chicken Little, and Chicken Little had been in the woods, and the sky was falling down!

We're going to tell the king.'

So Gander Lander joined Goosey Loosey and Drakey Lakey and Ducky Lucky and Cocky Locky and Henny Penny and Chicken Little, and off they went to tell the king that the sky was falling down.

On the way they met Turkey Lurkey ...

'Where are you going, Turkey Lurkey?' said Gander Lander.
'I'm going to the woods,' Turkey Lurkey replied.

'No, Turkey Lurkey, don't go there! I was going to the woods when I met Goosey Loosey, and Goosey Loosey had met Drakey Lakey, and Drakey Lakey had met Ducky Lucky, and Ducky Lucky had met Cocky Locky, and Cocky Locky had met Henny Penny, and Henny Penny had met Chicken Little, and Chicken Little had been in the woods, and the sky was falling down!

We're going to tell the king.'

So Turkey Lurkey joined Gander Lander and Goosey Loosey and Drakey Lakey and Ducky Lucky and Cocky Locky and Henny Penny and Chicken Little, and off they went to tell the king that the sky was falling down.

On the way they met Foxy Loxy ...

'Where are you going, Foxy Loxy?' said Turkey Lurkey.
'I'm going to the woods,' Foxy Loxy replied.

'No, Foxy Loxy, don't go there! I was going to the woods when I met Gander Lander, and Gander Lander had met Goosey Loosey, and Goosey Loosey had met Drakey Lakey, and Drakey Lakey had met Ducky Lucky, and Ducky Lucky had met Cocky Locky, and Cocky Locky had met Henny Penny, and Henny Penny had met Chicken Little, and Chicken Little had been in the woods, and the sky was falling down!

We're going to tell the king.'

Now Foxy Loxy was a very clever and hungry fox ... so he offered to show Turkey Lurkey and Gander Lander and Goosey Loosey and Drakey Lakey and Ducky Lucky and Cocky Locky and Henny Penny and Chicken Little the quickest way to the king's palace.

But instead of taking them to the palace he led them to his fox hole!

Just as Foxy Loxy was about to eat them all for dinner, the **king's dogs** ran by barking and scared him away.

Turkey Lurkey and Gander Lander and Goosey Loosey and
Drakey Lakey and Ducky Lucky and Cocky Locky and Henny Penny
and Chicken Little all ran as fast as they could to get away from Foxy Loxy
until they finally reached the woods. As they huddled under a large oak tree,
the wind blew and acorns fell to the ground,

Plop! Plop! Plop!

Chicken Little looked up at the sky and realised that it wasn't falling down at all and that it was only an acorn that had fallen on to his head.

Chicken Little felt very silly for telling his friends that the sky was falling down.

But Turkey Lurkey and Gander Lander and Goosey Loosey and Drakey Lakey and Ducky Lucky and Cocky Locky and Henny Penny all learnt an important lesson that day – they no longer believe everything they are told without thinking for themselves.

The End